The Singing Hitchhiker
and
Other Stories

by

Susan Hutchins

I hope you enjoy these stories.

Susan Hutchins

**The Singing Hitchhiker
and Other Stories**

Text Copyright

© 2022 Susan Hutchins

All Rights Reserved

British Library Cataloguing-In-Publication Data
A catalogue record of this book is available
from the British Library.

ISBN 978-1-9160531-6-8

Published via pgprintandofficeservices.co.uk

Contents

Foreword

Susan Hutchins, author of the beautifully moving 'Skylark'
and 'Playinground', has turned to the short story form with
this new collection of stories, many of them inspired by her
experiences of growing up in Bristol, living and working
there and living in the West of Ireland. 'The Singing
Hitchhiker and Other Stories' is full of stories that feel very
real and authentic, sometimes poignant, sometimes with a
comic touch, such as 'An Affable Man', where a bored wife is
lured into a risky encounter with a dubious ex amid the
faded glamour of Severn Beach. These tales are very
evocative of the times and places they grow out of and make
for a very readable collection.

Tim Rhys, Playwright

The Singing Hitchhiker

Jack Jones was amongst the first of the passengers to leave Cork Harbour that morning. The weather forecast was diabolical and Jack was not looking forward to the long drive to County Clare. He'd probably been driving three hours, maybe more, when the grey sky turned to pewter and the first heavy drops of rain hit the bonnet of the car. Jack put on the windscreen wipers and reduced his speed.

After a few kilometres, he checked to see that all was clear then turned onto the Lahinch Road. It was then that he saw him – a tall, well-built man wearing a thick, brown overcoat, his shoulders hunched beneath his turned-up collar, his thumb held out hitching a lift. Jack had never made a habit of picking up hitchhikers; he preferred his own company. The few people he had given lifts to wanted to involve him in meaningless conversations or, worse than that, no conversation at all, which made him feel that he was the stranger in the car! But for some unknown reason, before he'd given it a thought, Jack pulled up next to the hitchhiker, rolled down the window, saying, 'I'm going to Miltown, if that's any help.' The man gave a nod, said thank you, and Jack waited for him to get into the car.

When Jack re-joined the traffic he asked the hitchhiker where he was going and was told that he was visiting his mother in Ennistimon. Ennistimon was another fifteen kilometres from Jack's destination, so he explained that he'd drop him off in Inna, as from there he'd get a better chance of getting a lift. For the sake of something else to say, Jack asked the hitchhiker where he lived. His reply gave Jack a jolt; even he knew how dangerous the patients in the psychiatric hospital could be! Jack began to feel nervous, cursed himself for the moment of sympathy he'd had for the man. He was wondering what his next move should be when suddenly the hitchhiker told him if it hadn't been for the singing he might have killed someone, and that it was the singing that calmed him. Jack gave the hitchhiker a quick glance then asked, 'So you sing, do you? That's nice. I'd like to hear you.' Jack hadn't expected to hear a beautiful baritone voice, or a song about the closure of the Welsh coal-mines. He had expected the lyrics to be the usual sentimental dirge he heard in the pubs. The never-ending songs about families forced to leave their homes, lost love and tearful reunion.

The hitchhiker was still singing when Jack parked the car on Inna's one and only road. He relaxed back into his seat, closed his eyes and listened to the miner's story. Jack learned about the miners' strike, how they and their families had suffered from hunger, insults and police beatings, and finally the loss of their jobs; how it made his own petty problems inconsequential. When the song came to its end there was a moment of silence before Jack heard the hitchhiker open the car door. He leaned towards him, thanking him for his song. The last Jack saw of the hitchhiker was when he drove past him standing at the side of the road, his thumb held out, hitching a lift.

The hitchhiker was still on Jack's mind when he'd left Inna. He wondered what drama had led the hitchhiker to the psychiatric ward and if his mother had been there to support him – the hitchhiker hadn't mention a father and Jack thought that, like his mother, she must be a widow.

Jack had just turned seven when his mother became a widow, but he remembered his father's funeral as though it were yesterday, the images floating in front of him like dusty cobwebs – seeing his uncle sheltering under a large black umbrella, watching a black hearse covered with wreaths parking outside the house, his mother walking down the garden path dressed in a long black coat, being told that the silver basket full of blue flowers held a note that said: "From Jack to his Daddy, never to be forgotten".

Jack had had to adjust to a new way of life. Without his father's wage, his mother needed to find a job. While she was at work Jack was put under the kind care of the next-door neighbour. Jack was no trouble to anybody. He was a dreamer; he conjured threads of what might have been: a game of football, a boat on a river, a red kite against a deep blue sky, his father's strong and capable hand wrapped around Jack's small one.

By the time Jack was fourteen, he wanted nothing more than to throw off his mother's apron strings and be free. At the age of nineteen he left college and was ready to leave home and find independence. He found a job in the automation industry, which led to an apprenticeship, which led to him living and working in Germany.

Jack's mother's one hope was that he would get married and give her grandchildren, but by the time she reached retirement age it had become clear that that was not to be. It was out of the blue when a solicitor's letter arrived saying she had had inherited an old traditional cottage in Ireland. Without giving it too much thought, she gave notice to her landlord, left her rented flat and moved into it. To begin with everything was fine. Jack would spend a couple of weeks with her each year. She had a large garden to tend to, was involved with the church and fundraising, and had made a group of new friends. It was a couple of years later when the garden began to be a chore, when the damp and rain began seeping through the cottage wall, stiffening her joints and slowing her movements, that she locked the cottage door and hurried back to England.

Jack hadn't wanted his life disrupted. He didn't know what to do with a homeless, ageing mother. He was a busy man; he didn't have time to be travelling from one country to another to visit his mother, and she would never have been happy living in Germany. She liked conversation and, at her age, how was she ever going to learn German! Jack earned good money and he thought the kindest thing he could do for his mother was to find a good care home.

Jack was nearing his destination when he thought again about the hitchhiker. He wondered if he'd managed to get a lift, if he was on his way to his mother, if there would be a pot of tea and maybe a Victoria sponge waiting on the table for him. Jack thought about his own mother. He couldn't remember a time he had shared a meal with her. The more he thought about his mother, the more he regretted his lack of kindness to her. She had made many sacrifices for him, and what had he done for her? Nothing that she would have wanted!

Jack knew he had arrived when the top of the slate roof came into view. As he got closer to the cottage, the more he noticed its deterioration: the gate hanging on its hinge, the faded paint on the front door, the cobwebs looking out of windows. Jack parked the car next to the peat shed, got out and looked around him. He saw how much things change when they are neglected: the grass that had been neatly clipped was a jungle of weeds, the paved path that should be under his feet, undetectable. Jack went to the car boot, took out the tools he needed and fought his way through the brambles and overgrown bushes to get to the back of the cottage. He tried to remember the spot where his mother had liked to sit and read. When he found the place he was looking for he pushed away the weeds and dug a small hole. He gathered a handful of stones and used them to spell out his mother's name. When he was satisfied with what he had done, he made his way back to the peat shed, opened the car door and very carefully took the urn holding his mother's ashes from the back seat. ▪

Stutter

When Joe died, the house fell silent. It was noticeable because Joe had been such a big man; big in every way: his body, his voice, his generosity, his overwhelming love of life, and all that went with it. Without him, the house is nothing more than a collection of rooms: a place to eat, drink and sleep; to look out of the window and watch the world go by. I've wondered if I should sell the house; let some loving couple enjoy it as much as we had. Whether I should take my memories and put them in another house and not look back – but looking back is what I've been doing a lot of lately.

I never wanted to cast my eyes on the years before I met Joe. I thought I'd sealed those memories and that they'd been forgotten. How wrong I was. The silent house has opened cracks, allowed names from the past to creep into my mind, made me look behind me and acknowledge their existence.

Before I introduce you to these characters, I must tell you about myself – I'd been the girl with the stammer, the one whose stutter wouldn't let her string two words together; a plain-looking girl just turned 15, inexperienced, unequipped to deal with the people who were about to walk into her life. The first to arrive was David. My widowed mother didn't know what she was letting herself in for when he put a wedding ring on her finger. Mum had been a proud woman who worked long hours doing a variety of low paid jobs to give us good food and a comfortable home to live in. She and I were innocents; we believed all men were as lovely as my father and granddad had been. What a shock it must have been when the day after the wedding Mum put on her coat to go to the pub with David and he said, 'Where do you think you're going!' Was it then that she realised things were about to change and the only things David wanted were his meals on the table and sex on demand.

I never said anything to Mum when David started trying to touch me where he shouldn't, when he whispered things in my ear that I knew were wrong – she had enough troubles to deal with. One day he went too far. It was then that I surprised myself, and him, when I told him with a voice as smooth as a purr that if he ever went near me again I would find a policeman and report him. I remember feeling very proud of myself that day. From then on David left me alone. I wasn't going to take any chances, and I started spending most of my free time in my bedroom.

It wasn't long after David moved in that I left school. Having what my mother described as an artistic streak, she arranged for me to train as a window-dresser with C&A – a fashion house in the heart of Bristol. I thought going out to work would take my mind away from what was going on at home; I'd no idea another aggressor was about to step from the wings, one that would show herself to be a master at threatening behaviour. They say don't judge a book by its cover, but when I first set eyes on Paula Smith I was struck by her beauty. She was everything I was not; my short, mouse-coloured hair plain and old-fashioned against Paula's thick, black ponytail; my skinny body a sliver next to her voluptuous frame.

For the next two years I was assigned to be Paula's apprentice – a daunting thought. I was in awe of her from the moment I first met her. It wasn't just Paula's good looks that attracted people; she was amusing, witty, and could tell a good story. Everybody liked her: management, shop assistants, cleaners, porters. There was always someone ready to stand and listen to her every word. It didn't take Paula long to know she had a plaything in her hands. A few kind words would have me believing she was beginning to like me; minutes later she would criticise my every move, leaving the little confidence I had in pieces. It wasn't just my work she found fault with; it was everything I did: the way I ate my food, the way I drank, my clothes, my hair. She tried to convince me and everyone else that I was taken on because I was simple-minded and that it was a requirement from the government to employ a few handicapped people like me. But what embarrassed me the most, what caused my face to become a furnace, was the mimicking, the laughter that came when she imitated my stammer.

My journeys to work and back became a refuge that was all too short – sitting on the bus, looking out of the window, living every stop, every start, feeling the minutes pass by, knowing the exact moment when C&A would loom up in front of me. The desperate need to stay on the bus, to let it take me to the very last stop, to catch another bus and another and another, would overwhelm me. But, of course, I had no choice. David was in charge of finances; the only thing I had in my bag was my bus fare and a sandwich.

I was mostly ignored by my colleagues, which was fine by me as it allowed me to work quietly on my own while listening to their conversations. They mainly talked about boyfriends and sex – I was ignorant when it came to boys. The few relatives I had were female and my secondary school was a girls' school. As for sex, hearing my mother's bed rocking and David's grunts through the thin plaster wall that divided us was more than enough to make me want to stay intact. During one of my colleague's conversations, Paula asked me if I had a boyfriend. When I told her I didn't want a boyfriend, she and her friends came to the conclusion that I was a lesbian – a word I knew little about. To save me from such a fate, they agreed to find me a boyfriend. I had no say in the matter, as the following day Paula told me she'd spoken to a male friend of hers and a blind-date had been arranged.

A new window-dresser had recently been employed. Christine was older than the rest of us; a quiet woman who kept herself to herself, so I was surprised when she came near to where I was working, took a quick look around her, then whispered she had something to tell me and to meet her after work in the courtyard of the old Wesleyan Chapel. I was already feeling nervous as it was the evening I was to meet my date. The only thing I knew about him was his address and that his name was

Dave. Curious as to why Christine wanted to speak to me only added another layer of anxiety.

Paula and her friends were far more excited about my date than I was. Their words of advice as to what I should say and do were lost in my wish to forget the whole thing and go home. As the day went on, I kept an eye on the time. When the hand touched six, before anyone could give me any more tips on kissing, I grabbed my coat and bag, and left. Christine must have been close behind me; seconds after I arrived at the Chapel, she was standing in front of me. As she delivered her message, my curiosity turned to horror. The man I was to meet in less than an hour was going to rape me! I don't know how long Christine stayed with me. I do know that after she left I stood for a while gathering my thoughts. When I felt able to leave the safety of the quiet courtyard, I went to the bus-stop, hailed the bus and took a seat on the left-hand side next to a window. I knew the route well: the stops along the way, the house on Gloucester Road, the one with the yellow door. If it hadn't been for Christine I would have got off at this stop. Would have gone to the yellow door and rung the bell.

That night I was fearful; there were sure to be repercussions. When I arrived for work the following morning, I waited outside on the pavement. At the very last minute, I went into the building and clocked in. I stood for a moment at the door to what we called the window-dresser's room. I could hear Paula's voice; they were talking about me! I knew I couldn't stay where I was forever. There was no escape. I was going to have to face them. As soon as my foot was in the room, Paula fired me with words, demanding to know why I hadn't gone to meet my date. Someone grabbed my arm and I saw I Christine leave the room. Hands dragged me towards the staff toilet, opened the toilet door, pushed me onto my knees and forced my head into the toilet-bowl. The roar of the flush, the deluge of ice-cold water made me gasp. I lifted my head, relieved to see they had gone. I stretched up my arm, felt for the paper-towels and pulled down a wad. I sat with my back to the wall, mopping my hair, wondering if life could get any worse.

The following morning, Christine didn't come into work. The news had spread quickly. It wasn't long before one of the shop assistants told me that, the evening before, Christine had been stopped from leaving the building, her bag had been searched and items of clothing from the store had been found. She was given instant dismissal. I had no doubt that it was Paula who had planted the clothes, which proved to be true; a few years later, Christine and I happened to come across each other. She told me what I suspected. Someone had planted the clothes in her bag and both of us knew who that person was.

You may wonder what was happening at home. I continued to stay out of David's way. He was a creature of habit and I got to know his every move – I knew what time he came home from work, ate his meals, the hour he put on his coat and went to the pub. My mother was the one who suffered, particularly at weekends. Every Saturday morning, before I left for work, she would ask what time I would be back. She was like a jittery puppet, her strings so cross-wired she was on the verge of falling apart. As I said, I stayed out of David's way. I recognised his footstep on the path, the sound of the drunken struggle as he tried to put his key into the lock. I had my own room to go to, but Mum had no such sanctuary. She probably thought I hadn't heard her muffled cries at night, or seen the ineffective make-up on the bruises in the morning light.

Nothing remains the same forever. I survived my two years at C&A then left and found a job as a window-dresser with a small chain of fashion shops. About the same time, my mother had one beating too many and she and I walked out of our home and rented a small furnished flat.

My mother had married David in what some call the good old days: when men ruled; when a tenancy had to be held by the man of the house. Luckily, David died a few years later and the council offered Mum a two-bedroom flat. At the same time, my life took a turn for the better. I enrolled at an art-class and Joe was my tutor. Joe never made any comment about my stammer; his presence relaxed me and my stammer faded to an occasional stumble.

* * *

I certainly never wanted Paula to come into my thoughts, but for some reason she has become rooted there, the things she said, the things she did as alive now as they were when I first saw her. Since Joe died, I've had an overwhelming urge to find her. Sometimes I dream of pouring ice cold water over her head; at other times I just want to ask why, what it was about me that made her so vicious. Paula won't be easy to find; forty years have passed since I last saw her. The only thing I know about her is that she once lived with her family in a suburb of Bristol called Fishponds. She may have married and changed her name. If that's the case, I'll never find her. I've searched online, looked for her on Friends Reunited, but Paula's name has never appeared. I'm just about giving up hope when I happen to be in Marks and Spencer and a woman catches my eye. I stop what I'm doing, put the dress I'm holding back on to the rail and take a backward step. I swear the woman I'm looking at is Judy Jonson, one of Paula's gang – her right-hand girl when it came to bullying. She's not the slim, young girl she once was, and her dark curly hair is streaked with grey, but I'm sure it's her. I think about how I'm going to approach her; then, putting on a smile, I go over to her and say, 'Judy! It is you, isn't it?'

She looks up from the shoe she is holding, stares at me for a moment then shakes her head, saying, 'Sorry, I can't place you.'

'I know you from C&A. You were a window-dresser. I'm Helen Brown. I was an apprentice window-dresser at the time.' It clicks. She looks around as though looking for a means of escape, and I say, 'Have you eaten? Let me buy you lunch. I'd love to know what you've been doing. There must be loads to talk about.'

I take the shoe from her and put it on the rack. I point to the cafeteria, saying, 'Look! There's a vacant table. If we hurry, we'll get it.' I put my arm through hers, steer her towards the table and hand her a menu. She looks around, and for one moment I think she's going to flee, then she sits down. I keep her attention by reading the menu out loud, encouraging her to discuss what she would like to eat. When we've decided, I go to the counter, returning with a tray of food.

It must be nerves that keep me talking. I tell her about Joe, how I met him, the things we did together. She gradually starts to relax and I ask her about her family. She tells me she has two daughters and five grandchildren, looks at me with sympathy when I tell her I was unable to have children.

It is when I come back with the coffee and she smiles that I begin to relax. I watch her sipping at her coffee; it won't be long before she stands up from the table, puts on her coat and says it's been nice seeing me.

I won't forgive myself if I let this opportunity pass by, so, trying to speak in an indifferent, nonchalant sort of way while hoping she doesn't notice the tremor in my voice, I say, 'Do you keep in touch with any of the girls from C&A?' Then, not daring to look at her, I hunt through my bag for a tissue.

When I look up, she says, 'Paula and I used to hang about with each other for a few years; then we both got married and went our separate ways. We kept in touch by phone, then that dwindled away, though I always send her a Christmas card.'

'Does she still live in Fishponds?' I ask.

'No. That was when she was single. She's been married and divorced twice since then. Over the past few years her health has become very poor and she's now in a home.'

I see a glimmer of hope and say, 'That's sad. You hear a lot of worrying stories about care homes. I hope hers is a good one.'

'It's the Orchard Care Home, not far from the old swimming-baths. A few of the staff got sacked. I think it's much better now.' She looks up at the clock saying, 'Gosh, is that the time? I must go.'

'So must I,' I say, standing up.

We put on our coats. She takes my hand, saying, 'I'm sorry you lost your husband; he sounds as though he was a lovely man. He's certainly given you confidence.' She goes to walk away, then turns and says, 'I'm sorry for the way we treated you.'

* * *

The Orchard Care Home is in a rundown part of Bristol, caught between the railway station and the now defunct old swimming-baths. Even with the sun shining, the three-storey brick building and its lines of small metal-framed windows is depressing; it certainly wasn't put here to be attractive. There are no shops nearby and any form of open space or entertainment must be at least a mile away. I guess most of the people who live here are in need of some form of care. Does that mean they have to spend all of their time in this out of the way place?

In front of the building is a car park. I join the couple of cars parked there, then I turn off my engine and look at myself in the rear-view mirror. Paula won't recognise me. When I tell her who I am she'll be speechless; it's then that I'll confront her with our past. I get out of the car. An empty plastic takeaway container has been left on the ground. I move it aside with my foot, smooth and straighten the skirt of my new cream linen dress. After gathering together my bag and the bunch of flowers from the passenger seat, I follow the concrete path to a reinforced glass door. I press the buzzer. The door opens and I step into a small reception area. I'm not here long before a woman in a pink uniform appears behind the desk and asks if she can help me. I've prepared myself for this moment, rehearsed the words I want to say, over and over again, but now I'm here I'm wondering if my acting skills will let me down. Certainly the spate of nerves that has suddenly taken hold of me won't help, so, forcing a bright smile, I say, 'I've come to visit an old friend of mine. I haven't seen Paula for ages. We used to work together. Back then I knew her as Paula Smith, but that was when we were teenagers. We both got married about the same time, but for the life of me I can't remember her married name.'

'We've only one Paula with us. What's your name?

'My name's Judy, Judy Jonson. Paula will know who I am straight away.' I hold up the posy of forget-me-nots and yellow primulas, saying, 'I picked these for her this morning; they're from my garden.'

'They're lovely; it's just what Paula needs. She's been a bit down these past few weeks. Put your name in the visitor's book then I'll take you to her. I'm afraid the lift's out of action so we've got a bit of a climb.' She waits as I write Judy's name, then we head for the stairs, her chatter going over my head as I hunt for ways to avoid us going into Paula's room together. I'm still thinking of how to deal with the problem when we turn into a long narrow corridor, lined with plywood doors, each one displaying the resident's name. My eyes rest on each door. When I read Paula's name, I start to worry; then, much to my relief, I'm told, 'I'll pop in and tell her you're here.' She gives a quick knock and disappears into Paula's room. I hear the sound of what might be a television and take a step towards the open door. Someone turns the sound off and I hear my escort say, 'I'll tell her to come in then.' I take a backward step. 'Paula's ready to see you,' she says. 'It's going to do her the world of good. Would you like tea brought in?'

'Not for me, thank you. If Paula wants one, I'll save you the trouble and go down and get her one.' I watch her walk away. As soon as she's out of sight, I go into Paula's room.

The first thing I see is the wheelchair; sitting in it is an overweight woman with her leaking, bandaged leg resting on a padded stool. Thinking there's been a mistake, I open my mouth to apologise. It's then that I hear a voice from the past say, 'Who the hell are you? Where's Judy?'

The voice throws me back through the years, slips me into the fifteen-year-old girl I had once been. I thought I'd cast that girl aside a long, long time ago. How wrong I was. Suddenly she and I are one. It's when I hear a confident voice saying, 'I'm Helen Brown. I was your apprentice window-dresser in C&A,' that I realise that not only did luck play a big part in my life, it is experiences that influence and shape us.

Ignoring the urge to move the net curtain, to open the window and let in some air, I turn away from Paula and place the flowers I'm holding onto the washbasin. I give a quick glance around the small cluttered room, noticing the single bed, the television, the photograph of laughing children on the wall; any other place or time I would have wanted to talk about the children. When I hear Paula's not-so-bold voice say, 'What are you doing here? What do you want? Where's Judy?' I look at her and say,

'I don't know where Judy is now. I met her in Marks and Spencer a couple of weeks ago. We had lunch together. She told me you were here, which was very helpful as I've been looking for you for quite a while.'

She turns and reaches for the emergency cord; I quickly move it out of her way. Looking worried, she asks, 'What do you want?'

I hesitate for a moment. What do I want? Seeing Paula as she is now has muddled my plans. Judy did say Paula's health wasn't good but I didn't expect to see her like this. It's one thing to confront someone who can stand on her own two feet, another when that person is so obviously unwell. With no other choice than to let the better side of my nature take over, I say, 'I'm not going to hurt you, though there's been plenty of times when I've dreamed of pouring ice cold water over your head. I've a bottle of tonic in the car but, don't worry, I'm not going to waste it on you; I need it for the gin.'

I was hoping my words would bring a smile, but it was a stupid joke and I'm not surprised by her stony expression, or when her voice, as sharp as a knife, demands, 'I shan't ask you again. Tell me what you want or clear off.'

Feeling I'm about to lose the battle, I quickly say, 'I want to know why you treated me the way you did. What it was about me that made you make my life so unbearable?'

Paula is obviously in no hurry to answer my question, and I can understand why; she probably finds my visit entertaining. When I leave here, it's likely she'll be left on her own. I watch a smile creep across Paula's face, wait expectantly for her to say something.

'It was your stammer. It drove me mad. Having to stand by waiting for you to get to the end of a sentence was not only irritating, it was embarrassing. The only way to shut you up was to mimic or laugh at you.'

I didn't know what I was expecting, but it certainly wasn't this. 'So was that it! My stammer annoyed you!'

'No. Not just that. You were pitiful, always trying to please. If we'd asked you to jump off a cliff you would have. I saw you with your mother once; there you were, arm in arm, as though you were a couple of mates. I bet it was the same with your Dad. That's what happens when there's just the one; doting parents never want their little darling to grow up. Couldn't you see we wanted to help you? That you needed to toughen up and find out what life was all about? Bloody Christine; if she hadn't interfered, you would have grown up a lot quicker. Dave would have taught you a thing or two.'

'Dave?'

'Your date.'

I look at her open mouthed. 'He was going to rape me!'

'I wouldn't call it rape; I'd been with him myself a few times. He could be quite the gentleman.'

For a moment I'm speechless. Having to put her right, I say, 'You have the wrong impression of my home life. It was never like that. My stepfather was violent and my mother spent most of her time trying to please him so she could escape a beating.'

I didn't expect her to question me, am surprised when she says, 'Did he ever attack you?'

'No. I kept out of his way.'

'You were lucky. I didn't have a stepfather. It was my father that ruled. My mother kept her mouth shut, too frightened to say a word, but she knew what was going on. She knew he was coming into my room at night and what he was doing.'

Shocked at what I'm hearing, I put out my hand, hastily dropping it when she growls, 'Don't touch me. I'm not after sympathy.' And then she tells me, 'By the time you started working with us, I was in a better place. My mum asked her sister to give me a home. I was thirteen when I went to live with her. She was a widow with three kids of her own. It wasn't perfect, but okay. In a way, things like that equip you for the world, especially when it comes to men. It teaches you to be on your guard, not to let them get the better of you. I've had plenty of good times though, especially when the kids were small. I don't see much of my son, but my daughters come when they've got the time and sometimes the grandchildren will pop in.'

'Do you like living here?'

'Now we've got new staff things are better, though there's not enough of them; they're often rushed off their feet.'

'Do you see much of your neighbours?'

'You don't half ask a lot of questions. If you must know, I see them at meal times; we usually eat down in the dining room but the lift broke down this morning, and those of us that need it have to stay in our rooms. There's a sort of garden out the back with a few potted plants and some chairs to sit in. A few of the residents like to go out there and have a fag. I gave up smoking years ago because of my chest, but it's not only that; I can't be bothered with all the gossip. I'd rather keep myself to myself.' She takes a deep breath, yawns, then says, 'I'm glad you came. I haven't enjoyed myself so much for a long time. Anyway, I've had enough of digging up the past; it's best left where it is. All this talk has made me tired, so I'll say goodbye.' Then she closes her eyes.

I stay looking at her as I go over what she has told me. Our lives had been very similar in some ways and I'm wondering if... that perhaps... that maybe she looked at my pitiful face and saw herself. Paula hasn't moved; her eyes are shut tight. I suspect she's awake, but it's clear that any further conversation is not going to happen. I put the emergency cord back to where it was, pick up my bag and leave Paula in peace.

I walk along the corridor thinking about the quiet lives being played behind each door, the past dramas, the loves and the losses. I reach the ground floor. A stack of tools are next to the open lift door. Two workmen are craning their necks as they look up into the shaft. I walk past them into reception. The woman in the pink uniform is sat on a stool, her head bent over a magazine; when she hears me she looks up and asks, 'Are you going already? That was quick.'

'Paula was tired so I thought it was best that I left.'

'Oh, that's a shame.' She pushes the visitor book towards me and asks me to sign myself out. Remembering to write Judy's name, I do as I'm told. She presses the button, the door opens and I step outside.

I take a breath of fresh air, enjoying the warmth of the sun on my face and walk back to the car. Having been with Paula, knowing I've a garden and a spacious house to go back to makes me begin to appreciate what I've got. The visit to Paula may not have gone entirely to plan but I met my objective. The preparations – the new clothes, the trip to the hairdresser were all done for a reason. If things had gone a differently I would have gone further, would have told her about my success as an artist, the holidays abroad, the beautiful house I live in. The truth is, all those things were nothing more than props. What I wanted, more than anything, was for Paula to know that little Helen Brown, despite her stutter and the bullying she suffered, has done very well for herself.

As I drive through the traffic I think back to Joe's last five months. Watching the cancer destroy him is something I'll never forget. When he died I was lost. A huge part of me had disappeared. I'd felt myself falling into a deep dark hole that I couldn't, and wouldn't, get out of. Joe had been my partner, my teacher, my friend, my lover. I thought we would go into old age together. Nothing was ever going to replace Joe. The thought of the emptiness in front of me whipped up a storm, fuelling an anger that had nowhere to go. That's when David and Paula came into my mind. David has been long gone, but I'd thought, however small, there might be a chance of finding Paula.

I look back further, back to the days when Joe and I were much younger. I never wanted to point my finger at Joe, but there were cracks even then, cracks that I chose to ignore. Seeing Paula, seeing the photograph on her wall made me admit to myself that the angry cloud walking behind me had set its sights on Joe. I find it difficult to be negative when I speak about Joe, and these words are going to be hard to say, but say them I must. I had desperately wanted a child. Doctors could find no reason why I couldn't conceive. We tried IVF, and every time it failed. I wanted to adopt; I knew there were many children who were waiting for a loving home, but Joe was adamant; he said he couldn't love a child that wasn't his. I have to say, I was compliant. Maybe if I hadn't loved him quite as much, I would have argued my case. ■

Michael Mahoney

Michael Mahoney's tractor arrives with the dawn; it trundles down the lane, passes beneath my bedroom window, reaches a crescendo with the clang of the farm gate, the low of cattle and the bang of the milking shed door. I look at my husband lying next to me, still unconscious from last night's binge.

All year round Michael Mahoney works his fifty acres of bog; he tends his fifteen skinny cows, cuts his peat, clears his ditches, swings his scythe, stacks his hay, scrapes the mud from the yard while curses fly through the air. What does he get from this? Half an ounce of tobacco and a piss-up in the pub on a Saturday night.

Once I can decipher Michael Mahoney's Galway accent, he and I become acquainted. He comes into my garden uninvited – land is land to him. He wants to know what I'm planting. 'Garlic,' I say.

'Garlic!' he replies 'They eat that in France.'

'Yes, over there,' I say, pointing to a direction where I think it might be. Michael Mahoney's main meal of the day is meat, potato and cabbage. Courgettes, runner beans, sweetcorn and garlic are as foreign to him as the man in the moon.

Michael Mahoney's wife is as thin as a whippet. She cleans the butcher's, the baker's, the chemist and the undertaker's after a funeral. Michael and his wife have three daughters and a son. The girls have emigrated to England; the boy is studying to be a doctor. A farmer's life is not for them.

It's not the slate tiles being whipped by the wind, the rain hammering at the window or the mud hobbling my boots that drives me back to England. It's the sight of my husband wiped out by alcohol, too tired and depressed to pick up his fiddle.

A phone call tells me my husband has pancreatic cancer; the prognosis is twelve months. I make the little bedroom next to mine comfortable. He will stay with me until he dies then I will go back to Galway.

Galway City is as I left it. The same can't be said for the house. At the first opportunity the damp jumped right in, embracing whatever it touched. I go to the window and look out at the garden. The paths have disappeared; the brambles are shoulder high. I go outside to assess what needs to be done. I hear someone coming and look round. 'I saw your car,' says Michael Mahoney's wife. 'Welcome back.'

'Sam died,' I tell her.

'I'm sorry, but I'm not surprised. He looked awful ill after you left.'

'How's Michael?' I ask.

She shakes her head. 'Not well; there's been trouble. It happened Christmas Eve, the one before last. Michael poured petrol across the kitchen floor and onto the hallway. I rang the O'Learys; they came running. They had to wrestle him to the ground. Someone called the Garda. It didn't take long before they arrived and took him away; six months he was in Galway Psychiatric. He's home now. As long as he takes the tablets, he's alright.

We're down to six cows now; it gives him something to do. When he doesn't come home I expect to see him hanging from the rafters. I blame it on his brother; we didn't expect Patrick to turn up demanding a plot of land to build a house on, not after all this time. The last time we'd seen him was at Mammy's funeral, and that was over five years ago. Patrick left for England when Michael was fifteen. The Daddy was dead so Michael took over the running of the farm and looking after Mammy. Patrick wouldn't settle for any old plot; he wanted a sea view, so he took the field we put to pasture, the one with not a bog-weed in sight, the one next to our bungalow. Michael couldn't say no; Mammy didn't leave a will. Patrick said he'd take half the farm if Michael didn't give him the field. Patrick built himself a mighty grand house; it makes our bungalow look like a cabin. In front of the house he's put a life-size concrete donkey; next to the donkey is a life-size concrete waggon; inside the waggon are two concrete men drinking from flagons. The grass grows tall between the donkey's legs and the waggon's wheels. Patrick rides a sit-on mower; I sometimes watch him drive it up and down, round and round. He throws the cut grass into the ditch. Everyone laughs when they pass Patrick's house; they say if the donkey was real Patrick wouldn't have to spend all that time sat on a mower. I ask myself why it was our house Michael wanted to burn down. For sure, it should have been Patrick's.'

I don't know who started crying first, Michael Mahoney's wife or me. I saw the tears rolling down her cheeks and knew they mirrored mine. ■

A Child's View

August 1954.

Hello. My name is Susan, but everybody calls me Sue. I'm nine years old, and in two months and five days' time I'm going to be ten. Today is Saturday. The summer holiday has just started and I've got a whole six weeks with no school. I'm waiting for my Aunty Flo, Uncle Jim and Cousin Alice to arrive in their car. They've got a caravan in Brixham, in Devon. Every year I go with them for a whole two weeks' holiday. When they get here, Mum will invite them in for a cup of tea, but they won't come in. They never do, because they're always in a hurry, saying things like, 'We must get on. We've got a long drive. The weather might change; we don't want to get there in the dark,' then Aunty will look at Uncle Jim; he'll nod and put my case in the boot. Mum will put her arms around me, give me a kiss and wait while I kiss my little sister, then she'll take Penny's hand. We'll leave the front garden. I'll get into the car, and Mum and Penny will wave me goodbye.

I'm not silly. I know why they want me. Alice hasn't got a sister, or a brother; when you go to the seaside you need someone to play with, and that has to be me. Some people are luckier than others. Luck can change your whole life. Like, if Penny was born before me, she'd be going to Brixham. If Aunty Flo didn't have a caravan, none of us would go to Brixham. If Dad hadn't died, we'd have bought our own caravan and gone wherever we liked. Mum cries a lot; she misses Dad. The only thing that would make her happy is if Dad was alive, and that's not going to happen. She worries about money, which is why she says things like, 'Money won't grow on trees,' and, 'I don't know where the next penny is coming from.'

Uncle Jim is the driver; I'm sat behind him. Every year I notice his hair getting thinner and greyer. Now he's got a bald spot right in the middle of his head. If I was sitting behind Aunty, I wouldn't have to keep looking at it, nor would it be me she looks at when she turns and asks, 'Are you alright girls? Why don't you play a game?' There're not many games you can play in a car. To keep her happy, we play "I Spy". It's not long till we run out of things to spy so we start counting how many cows we can see, how many sheep, which is all a bit boring. If we were in a different country, there'd be all sorts of animals to count, like kangaroos and monkeys. Alice has stopped counting. She puts on her grumpy face and, without saying a word, is looking out of the window. I always feel it's my job to keep her happy, but when she gets like this there's nothing I can do about it.

I don't mind being left to myself; I quite like it. I can think about the holiday and the things I want to do. One of the things is window-shopping – well, that's what Mum calls it. Every year I try to find her and Penny a nice present, but the trouble is the nice ones are the most expensive and the holiday money Mum gave me has got to last two weeks. Mum says it's the gift that counts and if I brought back a pebble she'd love it, but it's not the same as a real present.

Some days we spend our whole time on the beach and don't spend a penny. One of my favourite things is crabbing – there're two crab-nets under the caravan that belong to me and Alice. Because we come to Brixham every year, we know all the best rock-pools. All sorts of things live in a rock-pool: limpets, crabs, fish with big heads called blennies; there're lots of little shrimps, but you can never catch them because they're so quick. Everything we get goes into our buckets, but not for long. When we've shown them to the adults, we put them back in the rock-pool they came from. Last year we went on a boat trip; it was a proper boat with an engine, a captain and men working on it. Me and Alice stood on the deck. We felt the boat moving under our feet. We waved a goodbye to the people on the beaches, watched them getting smaller and smaller as we went further and further out to sea. Being on the boat was the best thing I've ever done!

If it wasn't for the problem, Brixham would be the most perfect place ever. The problem isn't about missing Mum; it's much bigger than that – it's about religion! Aunty Flo's religion is Pentecostal. Mum's is High Church of England. Mum and Aunty both say there's one God and his name is Jesus. What I don't understand is why they keep arguing about him. Aunty says that Jesus doesn't like the incense, the hymns, the vicar's robes, even statue of the Virgin Mary, and I think she's beautiful. Mum hates Aunty's religion. She says

Pentecostals are too righteous for their own good, that she'd love to push Aunty's religion right down her throat. I wouldn't mind them arguing if I wasn't in the middle of it. Aunty Flo wants me to be saved because she says if I'm not I won't go to heaven. Every time I go away with Aunty, Mum makes me promise not to let her save me. I really don't want to go to hell, nor do I want to be saved, because Aunty will tell Mum and that would cause one hell of an argument.

Alice goes in and out of moods quicker than anybody I know. One minute she's looking out of the window and not speaking to me, the next she turns and asks if I'm hungry. It's ages since I had breakfast so I give her a nod. She taps her mum on the shoulder and asks if we can have a sandwich. Uncle says he'll pull over when he can, and it's not long before he turns off the big road and drives into a tiny village that Aunty calls a hamlet. Uncle parks the car near a duck pond. Aunty takes the wrapped sandwiches out of the boot and we sit on a bench. I love ham sandwiches; they're my favourite and I'm wondering if ham is made in hamlets. We don't have much ham at home because it's expensive. I know ham comes from pigs and that Mum puts pigs' trotters in the stew, but they don't taste or look anything like ham. The ducks are quacking to say they want something to eat; the birds are chirping as if they're hungry as well. That's another thing about luck. Where you're born can be lucky or unlucky. You're not lucky if you're born in Bristol; there's nowhere to play because the rows and rows of houses get in the way. When I grow up I'm going to make my own luck. I'm going to get a good job, earn lots of money so I can buy a house for me, Mum and Penny in a hamlet by the sea, then we can live happily ever after.

We've been in the car for ages. Now we've gone past the small pink cottage with yellow roses around the door, I know where we are. I see the fast-running river and feel the up and down as we cross the hump bridge. We pass the big house with its wide gates and lots of grass and trees. We turn at the corner, go a bit further, and there it is: the sign that says "Welcome to Brixham". I sit up and look out of the window. Nothing has changed; the town is exactly how it was when we were last here. Uncle Jim does what he always does; he parks outside our favourite pasty shop. When he comes out he gives the pasties to Aunty and drives to the harbour. We sit on a wall eating our pasties, listening to and watching the waves hitting the sea-wall, the little boats bobbing in the water, the lighthouse in the distance. That's what I love about Brixham: it doesn't let you down, it wraps itself around you; it's what Mum calls dependable.

Uncle drives to the caravan-site. He turns off the engine and me and Alice quickly jump out. Nothing too much has changed; the caravan's pale blue is a little paler and one of the red curtains has a small hole in it. The cream enamel jug we use for getting water has been left outside and is full to the top with rain and green slime. Aunty opens her purse and takes out the key. She climbs the three wonky steps, fiddles with the lock and opens the door. We follow her inside – as always, the same musty smell is waiting for us. Aunty pulls back the curtains. Uncle brings in the cases then goes back outside to turn on the gas-canister. Aunty empties the green jug onto the grass, takes it down to the tap and brings it back clean and full of drinking water. She tells me and Alice to go to the toilet block and wash our face and hands. When we get back, it's starting to get dark. Uncle is lighting the gaslights and the soft yellow and the hum from the pipes fill the caravan with cosy smells and sounds. The two bunk beds are made up with pillows and blankets. We're so tired it doesn't take me and Alice long to put on our night clothes and get into bed. Aunty looks at us from the bedroom doorway; she talks to us about Jesus and the Devil and how the Devil can lead us into Hell – I know about Hell: it's a really scary place; you wouldn't want to go there. When I'm home we say the Our Father prayer, which is why I know the words off by heart. Mum's religion isn't the same as the Pentecostal's; we don't like talking too much about death and the Devil. We know about Easter and what happened to Jesus, but he wasn't on the cross long, and the story does have a happy ending.

I open my eyes and the first thing I hear is the screaming of seagulls, the flip-flapping of their feet on the caravan roof. I smell bacon frying and think of Mum and Penny and what their breakfast will be. While I'm having bacon, they'll be having porridge. Mum's porridge is yuck, even with lots of sugar on it. Penny hates porridge even more than I do. Sometimes she screams and cries so much that Mum takes the porridge away and makes her toast. If I was Penny I'd do the same, but being the oldest doesn't mean you can do what you want; Mum says part of the job of being a big sister is to set an example.

Sundays in Brixham are different from the rest of the week. Me and Alice can't stay in bed laughing and talking like we usually do. Straight away we have to get up, take our towels and soap to the toilet block and have a good wash. When we get back, the Sunday best dresses are laying on the bunks. My Sunday best dress is white with little pink roses around the bottom. Alice wore it last year and it's what's called one of Alice's castoffs. This year, Alice's Sunday best dress is pale blue with white embroidery on the pockets. I look at Alice's dress, seeing myself in it, hoping that next year it will be mine. I like getting Alice's castoffs because her clothes are really nice. I don't only get her dresses; I get her coats, her jumpers, her skirts, her cardigans and her blouses. When Alice's castoffs get too small for me, Mum puts them in the cupboard for Penny and then they become my castoffs.

Aunty has tied aprons around me and Alice. We slide onto the kitchen bench. Aunty puts a plate of food in front of us then sits next to Uncle. There's not just bacon on the plate, there's fried eggs, tomatoes and baked beans! This is my favourite breakfast, but I've only just put a bit of bacon into my mouth when Aunty starts talking about religion. All the enjoyment of eating is suddenly spoiled. It's not as though I can close my ears and not listen to her saying that Jesus is miserable when he listens to Church of England music and that when he hears Pentecostal music he's happy and smiling. Uncle usually doesn't say much about anything but this time he's agreeing with her, and even Alice has joined in and is laughing! I feel like I'm on my own. It makes me miss Mum, and I want to go home. Mum says we must treat visitors with respect. And that's what I am. A visitor! I wish I could argue with them but that would be called being cheeky, and it's one of the things Mum won't allow me to do, but If I was allowed I'd ask them how they know what Jesus likes and doesn't like, or what he's doing and thinking. Only the saints and a few others met him, and that was such a long time ago it would be a bit like playing Chinese Whispers: some of the story would get mixed up and forgotten. I really wish they would stop talking about religion. All I want is to enjoy my breakfast.

On Sundays we're not allowed to go to the beach, and the only book we can look at is the Bible! I won't tell anybody else, but I think the Bible is old-fashioned and really boring, and if they wrote it in ordinary language more people would read it. Sunday afternoon is the only bit of Sunday I like; it's when all the Pentecostals go to the harbour for music and singing. There's always a big box of tambourines for people to play with and sometimes there's a man with a guitar. I won't tell Mum, but I like Pentecostal music and songs better than High Church of England's music and hymns. I'd rather have tambourines and guitars than an organ that sends the old people to sleep. Me, Alice and the Pentecostal children like shaking tambourines and dancing. Sometimes we spin around so fast our dresses stand out like a ballet dancer's dress. I'm always sad when we leave the harbour because when we get back to the caravan, after we've had a sandwich and a cup of tea, it will be time to go to chapel. I'm worried – as soon as we get back, Aunty asks me to go for a walk with her. She never asks me to go for a walk, not just the two of us. I know it's something I don't want to talk about and I'm right. She's telling me I must go to the preacher and ask him to save me. I tell her about my promise to Mum. She doesn't listen; she's still talking when I burst into tears.

Aunty tells Uncle that we need to get to the chapel early. When we get there I'm the last to get out of the car. I follow them into what feels like a dark and scary castle. Aunty chooses a front pew, lets Alice and Uncle go in before her, then sits down. I sit next to her, wondering if she planned this to happen, that when the preacher asks the sinners to come and be saved, she'll give me a push. The people we met in the harbour are starting to arrive, all of them wearing their Sunday best – the children with clean faces and combed hair, the men carrying their trilbies, the ladies with their handbags over their arm. Everyone is talking, then suddenly the vestiary door opens and the preacher walks into the room. Everything goes quiet. Everybody is watching the preacher walk to the pulpit. I think about Mum saying she feels on the edge; that's how I feel, like I'm going to fall but I don't know where or when. The preacher looks down at us from the pulpit. He welcomes us into the house of the Lord, tells us that Mrs Jones has kindly offered to play the piano. Mrs Jones plays the introduction to "What a Friend We Have in Jesus" and we stand up. Some of the people have really loud voices, some just open their mouths and pretend to sing, some put their heads down so you can't see what they're doing. I'm one of the people that put their head down because I don't want to sing; the only thing I can think about is the promise and what I'm going to do about it. Mrs Jones stops playing and everyone sit down. The whole room is so quiet it feels like something big is going to happen, like a baby screaming or a bomb going off. Everybody is waiting. Everyone is looking at the preacher. Suddenly he opens his arms and shouts in a really loud voice, 'Are there any sinners here?' I look down at my lap, trying to make myself very small. 'Give yourself to God,' shouts the preacher. 'Only when you are saved will you find everlasting peace. Only then will you find a place in heaven. Save your soul now or be forever dammed in Hell.' The excitement is like the kettle getting hotter and hotter and all the steam is in the kitchen. I look up; people are leaving the pews, praying out loud, crying and asking for forgiveness. The preacher comes down from the pulpit, stands with his arms opened wide. People are going up to him and he puts his arms around them. I want to join them. I only have to go to the preacher and all my sins will be forgiven. It's only the promise that stops me. I think about Jesus, wondering if he loves Pentecostals more than he loves High Church of Englands. He said, 'Suffer the little children to come unto me.' Did he ask what religion they were? Did they have religions in those days? I think Jesus is kind, that he wouldn't want to send people to Hell. But what if the Pentecostals are right! Will I go to Hell if I'm not saved? Will Jesus understand if I tell him about my problem and all the problems Mum's had since Dad's died. Ignoring another push from Aunty, I close my eyes, thinking very hard about Jesus and what I'm going to say him.

Dear Jesus, I have a problem, and the problem is you. It's about religion. You see, my Mum is High Church of England and my Aunty is Pentecostal. Aunty wants me to be saved but Mum made me promise not to be saved. I don't want to go to Hell and I don't want to upset Mum because she says she has enough on her plate as it is. Dad died two years ago. We're much poorer now and Mum worries about money. I want to think Dad is with you even though he didn't believe in you or religion. I do try and be good; me and Alice did say a swear word but we did say sorry to you afterwards. What I want to say is, in case the Pentecostals are right, please, please will you save me.

I open my eyes. Aunty gives me a sad smile and holds my hand. The people who have been saved go back to their seats; the preacher goes back up the pulpit, and Jesus is telling me, in a very quiet way, that there's no need to worry, that the secret we share will remain what it is, a secret. ▪

A Box of Potatoes

Wondering where Paddy is, John casts his eye over the allotment. He'd told Paddy he was going to be delivering a box of seed-potatoes today. It isn't like Paddy not to be there when someone offers him something for nothing. He'd thought he'd find Paddy getting the ground ready for planting, or else squeezed amongst the assortment of garden tools in the little wooden shed, his flask on his lap, sipping hot tea from a plastic mug. John puts the potatoes down and tries the shed door. Finding it locked, he calls over to a woman who is busy digging a trench. 'Hi, have you seen Paddy?'

She stops what she's doing and looks up. 'No. I haven't seen him for a couple of days.'

'I promised him I'd deliver a box of seed-potatoes today,' says John, 'but thanks for your help. If you do see him, tell him I was here.' John considers whether or not to go home, then he reminds himself that the tubers need to be planted and, anyway, when Paddy's not on the allotment he's in the Red Lion. With that in mind, John picks up the box of potatoes, leaves the allotment and heads for his van.

Leaving the potatoes in the van, John pushes his way into the Red Lion. A gathering of pensionable, retired Irish men are sat at a table, their pints of Guinness at hand, nodding and shaking their heads as though something very serious is being discussed. John has met Paddy's mates more than a few times; he's listened to their grumbles about the British government, the reminiscing of the old days and the old ways, of an Ireland where the music and dance, Guinness and whiskey, potatoes and cabbage were, and still are, the best in the world. John walks over to them. Paddy is nowhere to be seen. They look up when John says, 'Hi, guys. Have any of you seen Paddy O'Connor? I was supposed to meet him at the allotment this morning. He's not there so I was hoping he'd be here with you.' They rest their pints on the table, look at each other, muttering, before coming to an agreement that Paddy had definitely said he'd be up at the allotment today. John thanks them for their time, says goodbye and leaves the pub wondering what his next move should be.

John sits in the van debating whether he should go to Paddy's place or home. He's been to Paddy's once before and it's not an experience he wants to repeat. It was back a few summers ago and late at night when John first came across Paddy. John had been making his way home from a Jamaican club where he'd been listening to reggae and smoking ganja. He was taking his time, strolling along, enjoying the night air, when he saw an elderly man lying on the pavement. John immediately bent over to see if he could help. The man's eyes were closed and John thought he was dead, then all of a sudden the man opened his eyes and shouted, 'Holy Mother of God; get me up from here will you?' John managed to get the man onto his feet. He would have left him where he was if he hadn't been about to fall again. He asked the man his name and address, and Paddy was sober enough to tell him. As John was going in that direction, he took Paddy's arm and led the way. When they arrived at Paddy's door, Paddy pulled a key from his pocket and immediately dropped it onto the pavement. John picked the key up, opened the door and saw Paddy safely into his room. From then on, whenever they happened to meet, John and Paddy would stop for a chat and very soon a friendship began to develop.

John decides to take the potatoes to where Paddy lives. Luckily, there's a parking place right outside the front door. Wondering why the door is wide open, he gets out of the van and takes the box of potatoes from the passenger seat. He walks into the hallway, puts the box onto the floor and looks around him. The house is so quiet John begins to wonder if anybody is in. From what he can see of it, the house looks neglected, as though it hasn't seen a vacuum cleaner or a duster for many years. The place is so depressing John begins to understand why Paddy needs to drink himself silly. Then, desperate to free himself from the potatoes, John lifts his hand and bangs on Paddy's door. He waits a minute, calls Paddy's name and bangs on the door again. For a moment, he's not sure what to do, and then he remembers Mick. Paddy sometimes talks about his next-door neighbour. He described him as an argumentative, miserable old sod, but having no other option John takes the few steps to Mick's door, is about to give it a knock when he hears a movement. Suddenly the door flies open and John guesses that the man with the bright red face, wearing grubby underpants and shouting, 'Holy Mother of God, what's the fecking noise about?' has to be Mick.

'Sorry,' says John. I didn't mean to disturb you. I'm a friend of Paddy's. I've been looking for him. I expected him to be at the allotment, but he wasn't there, nor was he in the Red Lion. I promised I'd give him a box of seed-potatoes. I've tried his door but there was no answer, can I leave them with you?'

'No, you can't fecking leave them with me. That box looks like it weighs a ton. And what if he don't want them? Then I'll be the stupid fecker who's got to get rid of them. Anyway, who let you in?'

'Nobody; the front door was open.'

'Bastards! How often have I gotta tell them to SHUT THE FECKING DOOR. Wait there while I put on my trousers. After I let you in, I'm gonna give Paddy a kick up his lazy ass!' He disappears, but within minutes he returns, struggling to pull up his trouser zip, grumbling to himself about Paddy, and wincing as he tries to straighten his back. John watches him pulling on a bunch of keys in his pocket then, cursing and swearing, Mick gives a sharp tug and the keys are in his hand. Breathing deeply and trying to get his breath back, he says, 'Paddy's fecking lucky to have me.'

John waits for Mick to recover then he picks up the box of potatoes and follows him into Paddy's room. Mick has only taken a few steps before coming to an abrupt stop. John looks for a place to put the box of potatoes. Finding no room on the floor, he balances them on a heap of newspapers. Mick is staring at a filthy, stained mattress. John looks over Mick's shoulder and sees

Paddy as he was when he first saw him – on his back with his eyes closed, wearing a scruffy grey jumper and a pair of worn out old boots.

'Come on, Paddy,' says Mick. 'What are you trying to do – scare the life out of us?' Kicking aside an empty beer bottle, he takes a few steps towards Paddy and, with the toe of his slipper, gives Paddy's boot a gentle prod. He looks back at John.

John squeezes past him, kneels down and puts his fingers to Paddy's wrist. A few seconds later he looks up at Mick and says, 'He's dead!'

'He can't be.'

'Well, he is.'

Paddy's donkey jacket had been thrown over a wooden chair; Mick lowers himself onto it. John pats his shoulder, saying, 'This must come as a dreadful shock.' Then he takes his phone from his pocket, saying, 'Do you know the name of Paddy's doctor?'

Mick shakes his head. 'He can't be dead here.'

'Well, he is. He's as dead as anybody can be. There's not an ounce of life left in him.'

Mick puts his elbows on his knees, looks down and shakes his head. For a moment, John thinks he is crying, then Mick looks up and says, 'He's gone alright. I can see that, and he needs a priest, but he can't be dead here.'

'One place is the same as another when you're dead.'

'Jesus, will you not listen to me? I told you – Paddy can't be found dead here! If anyone sees him dead here there's going to be big trouble.'

'Trouble for who?'

'His family.'

John opens his mouth in surprise. 'Family?'

'Yes, family. He's got a wife and her daughter living on the Southmead estate.'

'Well, I never knew that. Anyway, how will Paddy being dead cause them trouble?'

'Because he's not supposed to be here! You see, it's like this. His brother Tom had this room but then he got ill and the doctor put him on the sick. That's when Tom moved back to Ireland, and you know how it is. Tom's room was empty so Paddy started staying – mainly to get away from his missus. I tell you, she's a hell of a temper on her. When Tom's dole money kept coming, Paddy thought he might be back. He did try to get in touch with Tom but couldn't find his address. We, I mean Paddy, thought the best thing to do was keep quiet about the money and, well, you know how it is...'

'What dark horses you are!' says John, thinking how easy it is for Mick to transfer any blame for fraud or extortion right back to Paddy. Not that he blames either of them for getting a little extra on the side. Most of the Irish blokes he knows have worked their socks off for next to nothing. John would be the first to admit that he himself is no angel, that he enjoys a bit of wheeling and dealing; picking up something for a bargain and selling it on; working on the side, paying no tax and getting one-up on the thieving government. John ponders what to do next. He looks at Paddy, turns to Mick, and says, 'Is Paddy's wife on the phone?'

Mick shakes his head. 'I don't know.'

'Do you know where she lives?'

'I told you, on the Southmead estate.'

'Do you know where her house is?'

'Yes. I've been there twice. She kicked me out the last time I was there.'

'Good, that means you won't forget it.'

John pokes his head out of the door, looks along the hallway and up the stairs. After closing the door, he turns to Mick and quietly says, 'Do you know if there's anybody in?'

'Why are you whispering? They're not in, they're out. That's what they do when they lose their keys; they leave the fecking door open. Sometimes it's open all day. Do you know what I'm going to do? I'm going to bang that door shut so the feckers can't get in.'

'Hold on; I've got an idea. It needs a bit of quiet and that door will need to be left open. Paddy can't be here, so what we're going to do is to take Paddy back to his missus.'

'How...?'

'There's a yellow van parked near your door; it's mine. What I'm going to do is put Paddy in it. Your job is to stand outside and let me know if anyone is coming.'

'But what if someone does come? What then?'

'We hope for the best, and the quicker we move the better.'

John hurries Mick out of Paddy's room, along the passage and out onto the pavement. He opens the van door, then, leaving Mick keeping an eye out, he hurries back to Paddy. For a brief moment he looks down at him, sizing him up, deciding that the easiest way to move him is to put his arms under his armpits and drag him out. John also discovers that moving a dead body is not easy and that the phrase "dead weight" and "as stiff as a board" is a very true one. Worrying that any minute someone might come, John takes hold of Paddy while muttering, 'Death hasn't changed you a fucking inch, has it Paddy. You're the same useless, obstinate bastard you always were.' He finally gets his arms under Paddy's armpits then, moving as quickly as he can, he drags Paddy's body from the room, along the hallway and out onto the pavement. Not wanting to waste time by asking Mick to help him, and using his last bit of strength, he heaves Paddy's body into the back of the van.

As soon as the van starts moving, John heaves a sigh of relief, tells himself, 'So far, so good.' Then he asks Mick, 'What you going to say to her?'

'What? Say to who?'

'Paddy's missus. What are you going to say to her?'

'Nothing. I'm not saying nothing. She don't speak to me. Won't let me in the house. She blames me for everything – his drinking, his staying in Tom's room, him getting home late. She don't know about Tom's money; if she did, that will be my fault too.'

John pulls up at the side of the road. Leaving the engine ticking over, he turns to Mick and says, 'Well, what are we going to do?'

'You'll speak to her.'

John takes a deep breath; he could argue, but the only thing that will achieve is Mick getting out of the van and storming off. At least having him around might give some sort of support, even if it's only in the background. Before moving off, he says, 'How much further? What's her name?'

They park opposite a terrace of houses. Mick points to the one with the well-kept garden and the bright yellow door. John gets out of the van, crosses the road and opens the garden gate. Wondering how on earth he's going to break the news, he walks up the path and rings the doorbell. A net curtain twitches; a few seconds later and a large, blonde, middle-aged woman with an anxious face says, 'Yes?'

'Are you Mary? It's about Paddy.'

Her eyes widen. 'What's the bastard been up to? I've been sick with worry. Where is he?'

John points across the road. 'In the van, but...'

Before he can stop her, she marches down the path. He chases after her and grabs her arm. She pushes him away, shouting, 'Let me at him. The trouble he's given me. Two days I've been out of my mind, and...' At the sound of a car, she stops speaking and looks at the police car pulling up behind John's van. 'I've reported him missing,' she says. 'I'm going to look a right fool now he's come back.' ■

A Lucky Find

It was a lucky find – or was it? It was seeing the glint of gold in the stream that started it all off. I was curious, wanted to know what the shiny thing was, so I took off my shoes, slid down the bank and stepped into the icy water. That was when I stubbed my toe. Not wanting to stop for such a small injury, I ignored the pain and carried on. The water was now up to my knees, the bottom of my skirt floating around me. The shiny thing was within my grasp. I stretched out my arm, put my hand into the water, grabbed it and let out a yelp. I lifted the shiny thing into the air; a tiny bead of blood was sitting on the end of my finger. Putting my finger into my mouth, I looked at what was in my hand. I was holding a brooch. It must have been the clasp that had pricked me, but it didn't matter; the brooch was so beautiful, it was worth the loss of a little blood and the effort in getting it. I stood looking at it in wonder. The brooch was golden and in the shape of a heart. There were diamonds all around the edge and in the middle was the biggest, reddest, jewel I'd ever seen. The sun touched the jewel and it shone so bright it seemed almost unreal. I was still standing admiring my find when I heard Polly shouting her mouth off on the other side of the stream. I'd completely forgotten she was with me, so I turned to look at her as she shouted, 'That thing that you're holding is mine. I saw it yesterday but Mum told me not to go in the stream.' There's no way Polly saw it yesterday; if she had she would have told me, and there's no way she could prove it was hers, so I glared at her and slipped my brooch into my pocket with my fist closed tightly around it.

After a bit of name-calling between us, Polly put out her tongue and went off in a huff. I waited a couple of minutes to make sure she had gone then waded back across the stream and climbed up the bank. I pinned the brooch to the lapel of my blouse, poured the water out of my shoes, then flapped my skirt up and down to dry out before Mum saw it. I started making my way home, all the time thinking about my brooch, touching it to make sure it was still there. I was planning how it was going look when I added it to my collection of very special things, when suddenly I heard Mrs Higgins yell out my name – Mrs Higgins lives five doors down the road from us. I waited as Mrs Higgins marched towards me, took a step back as she crossed her arms and said, 'That brooch you're wearing is mine! I lost it when I was hurrying to get to the shops before they closed.' There was no way it could have been Mrs Higgins' brooch! She isn't interested in wearing nice things. She wears aprons every day and they're not pretty like Mum's are. Mrs Higgins' cardigans are out of shape and her slippers slop around her feet, so why would she want something as beautiful as my brooch. She started to get angry with me, and the only thing I could think of doing was to tell her the brooch belonged to my Mum. She went quiet after that, so I knew she'd been lying.

Some people say Mrs Higgins is an old miser and that she has a horde of money stashed under her bed. I never believed it but I began to wonder if they might be right, that Mrs Higgins knows the brooch is worth money and that is why she wants it. There's a jewellery shop in town and after a bit of thought I decided the best thing I could do was take my brooch into the shop and ask them to tell me how much it is worth. Before I went into the shop, I looked in their window. There were a lot of lovely rings and necklaces on display, though I'm pleased to tell you there was nothing as lovely as my brooch. I caught a glance of myself in a mirror, started to worry about what I looked like – I had mud on my skirt and my flimsy trainers were still soaking wet. I told myself that this wasn't about what I looked like, it was about my brooch, so I pushed open the door and went inside. Everything was calm and quiet; thick carpet covered every bit of the floor, and people were talking in whispers. I looked for the nearest vacant counter, went to it and unpinned my brooch. I'm only there a couple of seconds when a man wearing a grey suit and a shirt and tie came to my counter and asked what I was doing there. I didn't get any further than showing him my brooch and asking what he thought it was worth when the man burst out laughing and told me it probably came out of a Christmas cracker. Everybody in the shop heard it; they all turned to look at me. Every one of them had a smile on their face. It was definitely my most embarrassing moment ever and the only thing I could do was to turn away from the counter, hold my head high and, with my brooch in my hand, walk out of the building.

I don't often feel my face go red. I never told anybody what happened in the jewellery shop – some things are best kept to yourself – but now, when I look back at that day, I realise the brooch was a lucky find. The brooch is now safely in my collection and nobody will want it but me. Polly has found a new friend and won't bother me again and, hopefully, Mrs Higgins won't ask me to bring in her coal, mow her lawn or cut her toenails! ■

An Affable Man

Lucy Ann and her husband Ben had been living in Swindon for so long, most of the locals thought they had been born there. Everybody liked Ben; he was an affable man, a staunch member of the community - Tidy Towns - Street Warden - Church Warden - Swindon in Bloom, and eventually the elected Lord Mayor! Ben was a handsome man, upright, with a shock of pure white hair and a face that seemed to be always smiling. Everybody who knew Ben wondered what he saw in Lucy; she was his opposite in every way. Whereas Ben would be found around and about the town, doing things for people and chatting, Lucy kept herself to herself and doing what she called minding her own 'busyness'. There was nothing Ben wouldn't do for Lucy. Every morning before she got out of bed he took her up a tray of tea and biscuits. Every weekend he made sure she had enough money for the hairdresser, and anything else she may need. He took her out for meals. They holidayed abroad. She had wardrobes full of beautiful clothes. He even gave up alcohol to please her, despite the fact she sat down most evenings with a large gin and tonic in her hand.

Ben was blind to Lucy's true feelings. He thought she was content with their life the way it was, but there were things that Lucy found very irritating about Ben.

One was his optimism – she would have liked to have seen it crashing down on top of him. The other was his refusal to use the computer. Lucy didn't understand why Ben was so against the computer; he was a practical man, a mechanic by profession. He ran his own second-hand car business until the day he retired. When Lucy questioned Ben about the computer, he said he preferred to speak to people face to face rather than relying on a machine and, anyway, she was better than he was at choosing and booking holiday destinations and the short breaks to London when she wanted to see a musical or a concert.

Lucy never seemed to appreciate the care and attention Ben gave her. It wasn't that she was oblivious to what people thought about her – being disliked kept the nosy-parkers out of her way. If she was asked, Lucy would have had to agree that she was complicated, that there were times when she didn't know what she did want and what she didn't. Whether she loved Ben or hated him, whether she was happy or sad.

To delve a bit more into Lucy's character, I must take you back thirty years. Lucy was nineteen at the time and engaged to be married to a young night-club singer called Shane Fortune. Shane was good-looking. He sang and played his guitar in whatever night-club that would book him. Lucy didn't worry about Shane's lack of money. She was looking forward to sharing the fame and the good fortune his name was going to give them. That was until he ran off, taking Lucy's engagement ring with him. Lucy had been so shocked, so hurt and embarrassed at being jilted that she left a goodbye note to her parents, said nothing to her friends, and moved to London, where nobody would know her. Lucy has kept what happened between her and Shane strictly to herself; the only other person who knew about it was Shane Fortune himself.

It was probably boredom that made Lucy start up her computer and trawl through Facebook. She hadn't been conscious of looking for Shane, though he must have been on her mind, because his name appeared on her screen. She counted fourteen Shane Fortunes. The one that stood out had a face she recognised, a face that was etched with the marks of a life full of fun. Lucy's first thought was to delete Shane's name. At the same time, curiosity got the better of her and she requested Shane to be her friend. Shane accepted Lucy as a friend. Lucy gave Shane her telephone number and almost immediately her phone rang.

Shane's voice took Lucy back to her youth. Shane had never been serious about anything and she was pleased to hear the devilment was still with him, the search for the excitement and pleasure they once shared. Lucy was aware that Ben could walk into the house at any moment. Keeping an ear out for the sound of his car, she quickly told Shane she was married, that Ben knew nothing about their past relationship, and that was the way she wanted it to stay.

Lucy got in touch with Shane whenever Ben was safely out of the way. She didn't want to spoil her developing relationship with Shane by mentioning the engagement and the loss of her ring, so she put the conversation aside for another time. Speaking with

Shane, listening and laughing to the stories he told, the love songs he sang, the strum of his guitar made her feel alive. She was attracted to Shane's devil-may-care attitude, an attitude that took her away from the boring and predictable life she had with Ben.

The faster the weeks went by the more Lucy wanted something other than just talking with Shane. The next time they spoke she broached the subject of them meeting up somewhere. Shane was all for it, then Lucy went further and suggested they spend a night or two in a hotel. Shane raised an eyebrow at the word hotel and said, 'Why waste money when you can stay in my house? It may not be a palace, but it's perfectly comfortable.' Lucy loved staying in hotels but thought this time she'd let Shane have his way. They started to make plans. Shane told Lucy his address and how to get there. Lucy didn't know there was a small village called Severn Beach not far from Bristol. It sounded a nice place to be and she started looking forward to being in the country and enjoying the sea breeze.

Lucy began to wonder what she was going to tell Ben – she never went anywhere without him. Then she decided that nothing was going to stop her and all she needed was someone to cover for her. The only person Lucy was able to call a friend was Jill. Lucy and Jill had been flatmates soon after Lucy moved to London. They'd enjoyed many wild times together. Not a weekend went by without a party to go to, getting stoned, or one of them finding herself in bed with a man she didn't know. Then Lucy met Ben and she started enjoying the care and stability he gave her. When Ben asked her to marry him she gave him a positive yes, and within months she had left London and moved in with him.

Lucy's friendship with Jill had dwindled over the years, became no more than a few phone calls and a card at Christmas, but Lucy remembered the good times and thought Jill would support her in her little adventure. Lucy rang Jill and told her that she had met someone, a man she liked very much. They wanted to spend a night together and, in the unlikely event of Ben contacting her, asked whether she would cover for them. Lucy had expected Jill to join her in a giggle, and was taken aback when Jill called her stupid, said she had never appreciated Ben, and that most men would have left her years ago. Lucy wasn't used to being challenged. She was lost for words, and the only thing her brain could think of doing was slamming her phone down.

Lucy was determined. She'd made up her mind. Nobody was going to stop her from staying a few nights with Shane. The very next day she told Shane she wasn't going to wait any longer and would be with him in Severn Beach the following day. Bob was taken by surprise but pleased that he was going to have the house to himself. Lucy packed a bag that evening and was ready to leave in the morning.

Lucy's first impression of Severn Beach was one of disappointment. Everything about it appeared to be rundown. She parked her car near a rough piece of land littered with what looked like rusting bits and pieces from a defunct fairground. Across the road were a few shops. From the rubbish and litter on the pavement she guessed they sold food and drinks. A gang of kids were messing about, pushing each other and laughing. They noticed her watching them and she turned away, and saw a flight of concrete steps. Thinking the steps would take her to the sea, she climbed them. She had expected to look down on to a beach but all she could see was mud, acres of it, rivers of fast-moving grey water and a view that took her to what she thought might be Wales. Disappointed, she turned away and looked beyond the shops, wondering which one of the small, shabbily built houses belonged to Shane.

Lucy got back into her car and took the short drive to where Shane was living. She drove slowly, looking for his house number, then parked outside his door. Lucy couldn't help thinking that the word house was a rather grand name for something that looked more like a badly made chalet. Then, telling herself it was not up to her to judge where Shane lived, she knocked on the door. It was then that she started to wonder if she was doing the right thing. Shane had left her in the lurch, stolen her engagement ring and he didn't even have the decency to give her an apology. Then, before she had time to think, the door opened and Shane was standing in front of her. Suddenly her doubts disappeared. Shane's good looks were a little past their best but the character she knew and loved was in the creases of his grin, caught in the twinkle of his eyes. Lucy stepped into the house. Shane caught her in his arms and kissed her cheek. Lucy took his hand and followed him into what was a small kitchen-come-sitting room. Shane told Lucy there wasn't much to see but he'd show her around. Then he opened the door to a tiny bedroom. Lucy put her head into the room and looked at the single bed piled high with an assortment of what looked like old clothes. Shane told her she had a choice of two beds: the one she was looking at, or that she was welcome to share his. Lucy giggled, put her bag on top of the pile of clothes, saying the bag was happy, but she'd prefer to go where it was more comfortable.

When they went back into the main room, Shane invited Lucy to sit down. Lucy looked around her; there was a wooden chair with a tea-towel on it and a shabby two-seater sofa. Lucy sat on the sofa watching Shane opening a bottle of red wine. He told Lucy that all the houses in the row had originally been built as holiday accommodation, that back then Severn Beach was a thriving holiday destination, with a swimming pool, a boating lake, a fairground and a strip club. It was when people started going abroad for holidays that Severn Beach fell into decline. The strip club was the last to go; it had become a haven for drug dealers and prostitutes and a death nail for Severn Beach. 'But things are looking up,' he said as he handed Lucy a glass of wine. 'There's going to be a new housing development; all those rich people from Bristol will want to get out of the city for a breath of fresh air. They'll be queuing up to live in Severn Beach.'

Shane sat beside Lucy, put his wine on the floor, looked into her eyes and told her she had made his life worth living. As a thank you he had composed and written her a song. He pointed to the guitar, propped in a corner of the room and asked if she would like him to sing it to her. Lucy was too full of emotion to say anything. She watched Shane pick up his glass and finish what was left of his wine, and let her eyes follow him across the room. Lucy thought about Ben, his lack of passion or romantic feelings, how she had been starved of any love and affection. Lucy's eyes hadn't moved from Shane. When he came back with his guitar, she sat up straight, ready to listen to his every word. The song was good, but Lucy couldn't help thinking she'd heard it before.

Shane went from one song to another. The bottles of wine that Shane pulled out of the cupboard seemed to be endless. Night was beginning to settle and Lucy was bored. She had been enchanted with Shane's singing but had to admit there were times when anybody could have too much of a good thing. Lucy hadn't eaten since breakfast, not that she was hungry; the amount of wine she had drunk must have supplied her with all the calories she needed. Suddenly nausea overtook her and she ran into the bathroom and vomited into the toilet bowl. When she looked up, Shane was looking at her. He asked if she was alright. Lucy shook her head, pushed past him, opened the door to the small bedroom and fell onto the pile of clothes.

* * *

Lucy woke up with a thumping headache. It was daylight but she had no idea what the time was nor the energy to look for her phone. A shiver went through her and she realised she had fallen asleep with nothing but the clothes she came in. Her coat was on top of her but she couldn't remember putting it there. She cast her eye around; what she saw was a miserable little room, and realised that Shane was not going to give her the life she wanted. Desperate for a drink of water, she left the bedroom. Shane was asleep on the sofa, one leg on the floor the other dangling over the arm. Trying not to wake him, Lucy picked up a glass and crept towards the kitchen sink. As she turned on the tap, she heard Shane say, 'Make one for me. Milk and two sugars.' Lucy put her glass under the tap and wondered what her next move should be. When the glass was full she put it to her lips and drank it dry. She moved away from the tap and put the empty glass onto the table, looked at Shane and said she thought alcohol didn't suit her and if he didn't mind she was going to make her way home.

Shane stood up, saying, 'What! Just like that? You come into my home, drink my wine, get pissed, and would have left without so much as a goodbye.'

Lucy shook her head, saying, 'No, of course not. I wouldn't do such a thing!'

Ignoring her, Shane shouted, 'I know what this is all about. You were getting bored with your old man and you thought you'd get your claws into me. It must have been a disappointment when you found I wasn't as well healed as your Ben.'

'You don't know my Ben! You know nothing about him!'

'That's where you're wrong. The first time we spoke you told me a lot about Ben. He'd had his own business, selling cars. You told me about the charities he supports and him being Lord Mayor. For the sake of old times, you should give me a share of your good luck. Life's been a bit hard lately.'

Lucy was shocked, and shouted, 'What are you getting at? You won't get a fucking penny out of me!'

'In that case, I'll go straight to Ben. I bet he's got no idea you've been chasing after an old flame.'

'You wouldn't! Anyway, Swindon's a lot bigger than Severn Beach. You've no idea where we live.'

'That's not a problem. I've been online. It was easy finding the names of past Lord Mayors, and there's only one Ben on the list in Swindon. All I've got to do is to write Ben a letter saying what you've been up to, address it to the town council and they'll deliver it into Ben's hands.'

Lucy stood open-mouthed. She couldn't make up her mind if she wanted to kick him in the shin, hit him or pick up one of the empty wine bottles and break it over his head. ■

Golden Girl

From the moment his daughter was born, Harry had been in awe of her. When he gently took her from Pam's arms and felt the warmth of her small body against his own beating heart, he discovered what the word love truly meant. He'd never felt this way about anything or anyone before. He was so overwhelmed, he made a vow: his daughter would want for nothing. He'd work every hour he had to make sure she had the best that life can offer. Pam and Harry called their baby Rose, after a favourite aunt. It was when Rose began to look at the world with bright blue eyes, when her wisps of platinum blonde hair thickened to gold that Harry named her his Golden Girl.

Harry stuck to his vow, working every minute expanding his haulage business, hiring and employing until he had a fleet of juggernauts and an army of men. He never questioned whether Pam or Rose might like to see more of him – he felt a certain pride in the hours he gave providing for them. Pam and Rose had everything he thought a wife and daughter might want – a four-bedroom, architect-designed house with its own swimming pool; an acre of garden with a view of the Bristol Suspension Bridge; Rose with a place at Clifton College – one of the most expensive private schools in the country; a kitchen that any television celebrity chef would be proud of; a gardener to keep the flowerbeds blooming and the lawn weed free; a daily housekeeper to make sure Pam didn't end up like his mother – her good looks and spirit gone by fifty, worn out and dead by sixty-three.

Pam never complained about the amount of time Harry spent at work; she was happy with things the way they were, that the life she led was exactly to her liking. She didn't know what Harry thought about their relationship – they didn't talk about such things – but she was pretty sure that any romantic feelings they may have had died before Rose was born. Sometimes she wonders if she'd ever truly loved Harry, then she casts her mind back and has to admit that if there had been love, she doesn't know when or where it went. She's asked herself what she would do if Harry said he was leaving her, whether she would miss him or not. She doesn't need to think too long and hard about that question; the answer is clear: the only thing she would miss is Harry's money – and would she leave Harry for someone else? To that she could say a definite no! Pam's life suits her very well – she has a large circle of friends, can come and go whenever she pleases and she has her lovely daughter mostly to herself.

* * *

The years have gone comfortably by. Rose is now fifteen going on sixteen and is the apple of her parents' eye. She's popular at school, is liked by her classmates and teachers, and is doing well in her studies. What with two doting parents and a settled, comfortable home life, Rose feels no need to mess it up by behaving like a rebel.

The relationship between Pam and Rose has become so close that they are more like a couple of best mates. They spend most of their weekends shopping for clothes, going to concerts and the theatre, having the occasional trip abroad for a few weeks in the sun. You may wonder what Harry thinks about his wife and daughter's gallivanting. The truth is that Harry's more than happy to leave them to their own pursuits – there's no way he'd get on a plane as he's terrified of flying and, as for shopping, that's something women do. For the life of him, he cannot understand why anyone – including his own family – would want to sit with a load of strangers, listening to a concert or watching a play when you can turn on the television and enjoy it in your own home.

Harry thinks he's the luckiest man alive having a smart, independent wife like Pam. Every day he hears the men complaining about their wives' endless nagging.

* * *

The years have passed by without any unwanted dramas or upsets. Rose is now aged twenty-three and has been studying Marine Biology at Exeter University for just under two years. Rose has fallen in love and is desperate to tell her mother – she hasn't said anything to her friends as she wants Pam to be the first to know. Not wanting her friends to overhear, she finds a quiet spot, pulls out her mobile and dials Pam's number. Pam answers almost immediately; before she has time to speak, Rose says, 'Mum, I've some exciting news. I've fallen in love and I want you to meet him. You and Dad are going to love Paul, I know you are. Will you be free this weekend?'

Straightaway Pam is curious and tells her, 'I look forward to meeting him.' She doesn't say she's worried the love affair might be running ahead a bit too quickly. Then Rose says, 'I met Paul at a party... No, he's not a student at Exeter; he's at Guy's Hospital in London, studying to be a doctor. So that's fine then; we'll see you and Dad at the weekend.'

As soon as she puts the phone down, Pam begins making plans. Other than the gardener, cleaner and anybody that's been called in to do a repair, they don't have visitors. It's not that Pam doesn't like mixing with people, it's just that she prefers to meet her friends away from the house; that way she doesn't have to worry about providing a meal or entertaining. The need to talk to Harry about the coming weekend grows with each tick of the clock. Pam's tried to ring him a number of times but there's been no answer. Unable to sit still, Pam wanders from room to room, wondering what she will give them to eat, what the sleeping arrangements will be. She picks up the phone, is about to dial Harry again when she hears his car turn onto the drive. She puts the phone down, goes into the hallway, opens the front door, and watches him park as she walks towards him. 'What's up?' says Harry – Pam has never before left the house to greet him.

'I'll tell you when we get inside,' she says.

He follows her into the sitting room, stands listening to what she has to say. She waits for his reaction, then he shrugs his shoulders and says, 'Well, it was going to happen sometime, and if he's going to be a doctor he should be alright and he'll get a good income.'

As the weekend creeps towards them, Pam puts her efforts into organising how it will be. She has lost the art of cooking, not that she ever enjoyed it; eating to her is just an essential part of living, much like breathing, but Pam wants to make a good impression. She looks for a reputable firm of caterers and contacts them. Pam believes that the more you pay for something the better the service and product. The caterer emails Pam the menu. She looks down the list and puts a tick above anything that is expensive. Other than a glass of wine on birthdays and Christmas, Harry and Pam don't drink alcohol but, not knowing what Paul will be expecting of them, Pam looks down the wine list and orders three bottles of Champagne and three bottles of Beaujolais. Pam's table linen has been stuck in a cupboard for years and she now decides it's out of date. That very day she drives into town and comes back with a white linen tablecloth with matching napkins and two sets of designer bedding. Where the couple are going to sleep has been a dilemma for Pam. She is broad-minded but Rose is still Harry's Golden Girl, and encouraging some strange young man to share her bed will be a step too far for Harry.

The big day arrives. Pam can't remember the last time Harry took a day off from work, or the last time he wore a shirt and tie. They hear the sound of a car turn into the drive. Pam looks in the mirror and takes a last look at her hair and the new silk Monsoon dress she is wearing. She straightens Harry's tie and together they leave the bedroom. They make their way down the stairs. When they get to the bottom step they hear Rose's key in the lock. The door opens and straightaway Rose is in their arms. Rose turns to the man at her side and it's then that Harry and Pam look at probably the blackest face they have ever seen. 'I've heard so much about you both,' says Paul as he shakes Pam's hand.

Paul puts his hand out to Harry; ignoring it, Harry turns away from him, looks at Rose and says, 'Come into the kitchen; I want a word with you.'

Rose's smile has left her. She looks at Pam with a question hanging between them.

'You'd better go and find out what this is all about,' says Pam.

Pam waits for them to leave, then she looks at Paul and says, 'I'm sorry; I hate to say this, but I think your colour came as a bit of a shock. We don't see many black faces around here. You wait and see. Once he gets used to you, everything will be fine. Anyway, make yourself at home. Let me pour you a drink.'

Paul shakes his head. 'No, this won't go away that quickly and it probably never will. I told Rose there might be a problem, but she wouldn't listen. All she wanted to do was assure me I would be made welcome. I shouldn't have listened to her.'

Loud voices are coming from the kitchen; a door bangs, the sitting-room door flies open and Rose comes into the room shaking her head and saying, 'How could he, how could he. My own father is a racist, a fucking racist. I've got to get away from him, Mum.'

She turns to Paul, saying, 'Let's get out of here.'

She looks at Pam and says, 'Sorry, I know this is nothing to do with you, but Paul is not welcome and we just can't stay here.'

Part 2

There had always been a distance between Harry and Pam and it had suited them both, but the family has fallen apart and the distance is so wide they may as well be strangers. It would be an understatement to say Pam hated Harry; it goes much further than that. Harry's racist behaviour has destroyed any loyalty Pam once had for him; spoiled the loving and important occasions in Rose's new life – her marriage to Paul, the move to their new house in Dorset, the birth of their twin daughters. All of them, including his granddaughters, are a victim to Harry's cold and insensitive, exclusion – the children's loss of a grandfather, Pam's loss of a partner to share the joys of being a grandparent, Rose's loss of the father she once loved.

Every Friday since the break-up, as soon as it gets light, Pam picks up her travelling bag, leaves the house and drives to Dorset. Visiting Rose each weekend has helped keep their relationship as close as it's ever been. Pam has made sure she plays a big part in Rose's life. She was buying baby clothes as soon as she heard Rose was pregnant, was with her soon after the twins were born. Being able to see and hold her grandchildren is now the highlight of Pam's life. The two days Pam spends with the family are far too short and before she knows it she is packing her bag and getting ready to leave. Pam knows she is welcome to stay longer but doesn't want to outstay her welcome – she hasn't forgotten what it's like to be a young wife, with her mother hovering at her side, eager to take control.

From the moment Pam leaves Dorset her thoughts are set on Harry and her search for revenge. If anybody could hear the vicious and unhappy endings that Pam plots for him she would be reported and arrested. As she gets closer to Bristol, Pam's anger escalates. Seeing Harry's car parked on the drive kicks her into wanting to tinker with the brakes. Walking into the kitchen makes her yearn to pull the sharpest knife off the rack, find Harry and stick it into him. Luckily, so far, Pam has done none of those things.

Harry is well aware of Pam's feelings towards him, and he has had to accept the fact that she is never going to see his side of the argument. When he'd suggested to her that they went to church to grieve the loss of their daughter and that they should move to the country and make a fresh start, Pam had been speechless. Harry had never been frightened of anyone before, but that evening he honestly believed she was going to kill him.

Harry knows he is on his own with his views but, despite what everybody is saying, he still does not feel he is the one that is in the wrong; everything is the fault of his family – they are the ones that caused the break-up: Rose for falling in love with Paul, Paul for being black, and Pam for her coldness towards him, a coldness that he says has drained him of all his energy, the enthusiasm he once had for going to work, and caused the tiredness that renders him unable to lift his head from the pillow each morning.

Pam does whatever she can to stay out of Harry's way, but there are times when their paths cross and it's then that she notices his loss of weight, the yellow tinge to his skin. It's when she hasn't seen or heard him for a few days that she stands listening outside his bedroom door, wondering what she should do. After waiting a minute, she taps on the door and, hearing nothing, opens it. She walks into the room and looks towards the bed. Harry is lying on his side. She goes over to him and he turns towards her and says, 'Pam, you've got to help me. I've got terrible bellyache and I feel dreadful.'

Straightaway Pam goes to the phone and calls the doctor. Then she rings Rose and tells her, 'He looks dreadful. I can't possibly come to you and leave him on his own.'

'Why not? You don't owe him anything!'

'I know that, but the last thing I want to happen is to go home from you and find him dead in bed.'

'I don't know how you carry on living with him.'

'I wouldn't call it living. Anyway, I've told you – I own half of this house, and if he carries on looking the way he is it won't be long until I'll get all of it. Sorry, Rose, I'll have to go; the doctor's just arrived.'

A week later, Harry was diagnosed with liver cancer; the prognosis is six months. When he was first diagnosed Harry had been spitting with anger, blaming Pam and Rose for the stress they caused, the stress that led to his cancer. Harry's anger drained the last of his energy. It's then that he came to a stage where he gave up on life, submitted to the fact that he was dying and that there was nothing he could do about it.

* * *

Pam has employed a team of carers to look after Harry. She keeps away from him as much as she can but makes sure his bedding is clean and his food is to his liking. Rose has questioned Pam about her involvement in Harry's care; she wanted to know why Pam bothers with Harry when she so clearly hates him. Pam has to think for a moment, then says, 'I want to watch his decline. I want to see him suffer, to be there at his end; it's then I'll be truly sure he's dead and out of my life.'

No one comes to visit Harry; not that it matters – Harry was never one to encourage visitors. Pam does wonder who's taken over the management of Harry's business, who keeps the trucks in the tiptop condition that must be expected of them, who sorts out the wages, keeps the place clean and locks up at the end of the day. Until now it had never crossed Pam's mind to even think about what went on in Harry's working life. His work had been his domain and nothing to do with her. Pam is not worried about money; there is more than enough going into their banks each month, and she does have access to both his and her own bank account.

Pam hasn't failed to notice the fast deterioration going on in Harry's health. The word "funeral" has never been mentioned, and she's beginning to wonder if Harry is leaving all the preparations to her – if that is the case, she would be more than happy to put his body in a sack and drop it into a hole in the ground, though she wouldn't want to upset anyone, and there may be someone who might want to come round for a glass of sherry and pay their last respects. Knowing that organising Harry's funeral will be the last thing she does for him, she swaps the smile on her face for a sad one, goes into Harry's room and tells the carer on duty that she wants to have a private conversation. She waits for the carer to leave, then she sits next to Harry's bed and says, 'I've been thinking. Have you any thoughts about your funeral?'

Without a moment's hesitation, Harry says, 'I'm not having a funeral; I'm leaving my body to science.' He looks across the room and points to a chest of drawers, saying, 'In there you'll find the papers, signed and ready to go.'

Harry would never have guessed that his answer gave Pam a seed of hope; it was a small seed but, with a little planning and luck, it may give Rose a reason to celebrate. The more Pam thinks about her plan, the more eager she is to give it a try. Outwitting Harry will be the most difficult part to play, but she's lied to him in the past and he's always believed what she'd said.

Part 3

Pam rang Rose first thing in the morning. She told her she needed to speak with her but would rather not do it over the phone. She refused to tell Rose what it was about, only that it was a long story and she would be driving to Dorset later in the day and would tell them everything then. Pam's next step is to arrange cover for Harry. After she has done that she will make a quick visit to an old friend.

* * *

It is gone eight when Rose lets Pam into the house. Before Pam can say anything, Rose puts her finger to her mouth and whispers, 'The children are in bed.' Pam follows Rose into the sitting-room. Paul is opening a bottle of wine and he asks Pam if she wants a cup of tea. It's unlike Pam to want alcohol but she asks for a glass of wine instead and takes it with her to an armchair. Curiosity is written on Rose and Paul's face. They sit on the sofa and Rose says, 'What's it all about, Mum?'

For a moment Pam doesn't answer. She has gone over and over what she wanted to say and now she's here everything has gone completely out of her head. She takes a sip of wine, hoping it will give her courage, then says, 'I must begin at the beginning. I know it will sound as though I'm making excuses, which I suppose is what I am doing, but in my defence I must say I was young, hardly more than a child. Harry and I hadn't been married a year. I thought we'd be doing things together, but he was always busy with one thing and another. He made me feel I was in the way. I hated the job I was doing and wanted a bit of fun, so I started going out with a group of old school friends, to night-clubs and parties. I did try and get Harry to join us, but he was never into socialising. Anyway, one thing led to another and... and... well, this is going to come as a shock, but there's no other way to say it – Harry might not be your father.'

There is a second of silence before Rose says, 'And Harry has no idea?' – Rose doesn't call Harry "Dad" anymore.

Pam shakes her head. 'No, he doesn't.'

~ 72 ~

'Who is the man?' asks Rose.

'Don't ask me anything else at the moment,' says Pam. 'I've plenty more to tell you. When Harry donated his body to science I thought he'd saved me a job and then I got thinking. I thought maybe we could play a trick on him, so I told him the people who will be dealing with his dead body had been in contact and that they need a swab taken from him, that it's a way of checking they've got Harry Edward's body and not someone else. I told him there will be more information in the post, as well as his swab. The whole time I was talking to him I was a bag of nerves, but it worked; he fell for it hook, line and sinker. As soon as I knew I was on the right track I went to see a nurse friend of mine. She gave me a couple of packets of swabs and told me what I had to do. I did Harry's swab before I left this morning; it's in my bag, as well as one for you.'

Pam looks at Paul and says, 'This is where you come in, Paul. I've no idea where to go next.'

Rose is looking at Pam as though she doesn't know her. 'It's a way of finding out if Harry is your father,' says Pam.

Paul gives a big smile, puts his arm around Rose and says, 'Your mum's a genius. I'm working at the hospital tomorrow morning. I'll take Harry's and Rose's swabs with me and we'll have an answer by the afternoon.

* * *

Pam and Rose are standing at the bay window, looking out at the garden; a swathe of daffodils has given the ground a deep carpet of gold. The sitting-room floor is covered with children's toys; the only sound is their laughter as they sit on the floor watching "Mr Tumble". Paul's car appears on the driveway. Rose goes into the hallway and lets him in. Pam turns to look at them when they walk into the room. She knows from the smile on their faces the result is what they want.

'So, now you can tell me, Mum. Who is he?'

Pam looks at the twins, longing to hide her face in the softness of them. She lifts her head and says, 'I don't know who he is. We didn't take anything seriously back then. It was so long ago I can't even remember their names. I'm sorry.'

'There was more than one?!'

Pam nods. At the same time "Mr Tumble" comes to an end. The children crawl over the carpet to Paul. He picks them up, holding them in the crook of each arm. Rose looks at Pam and says, 'Maybe it's for the best, Mum. I have all I want here. If we go searching the past, we might open a can of worms.' ■

Dot

I first met Doris Ann Smith when she was living with her mother in a council house on the outskirts of of Bristol. She and I went to the same girls' school. One of the things she hated more than anything was being called Dot. She thought it was a belittling word that made her feel she was a nothing person, a dot on the page, a dot that was so quiet and small nobody would know she existed. She blamed her mother for the name problem. After all, it was her mother who chose the names; her father walked out of their lives before Dot was born. Those of us that knew Dot well couldn't help noticing how controlling her mother was. Dot could do nothing without asking her first. It wasn't as though she wanted a lot, just the ordinary, simple things that teenagers were attracted to, such as back-combing their hair, or choosing the clothes they wanted to wear, but Dot's mother didn't like the modern look, such as bouffants and short skirts. She had even threatened to take Dot's clothes, build a fire in the garden and burn them.

Dot had been so protected by her mother she didn't have a clue about what had happened in the world; she certainly knew nothing about boys! Things did change for the better when Dot left school and started working in the factory. The girls she worked with talked about sex whenever they had the chance, and Dot certainly learned a lot from them. There was one boy Dot did like. He was nearly always waiting at the bus-stop in the mornings. He would insist Dot got onto the bus before him. If the seat next to her was available he would sit beside her; if the bus was full he would get close to wherever she was, grab anything to hang on to and chat non-stop. One morning he asked Dot her name. The question was so sudden she didn't have time to think about any other name but her own. He told her he liked the name Doris – which made Dot wonder if he said it to be kind. Then he told her his name. Dot thought the name Bob suited him perfectly; it was a nicely rounded name, not a film-star kind of name, but a smiley, friendly name on a face she could trust.

Boys were a mystery to Dot. Her secondary school was all girls and her family were mostly female – she had one Aunt, three girl cousins and an uncle she seldom saw. When Bob started to talk to Dot she'd been almost too shy to answer him, but bit by bit and day by day she began to creep out of her shell and started to look forward to seeing him. Over the coming weeks their friendship progressed and it wasn't long before the most exciting thing happened. Bob had got onto the bus, sat beside Dot, and said, 'My mum's going to my sister's for the weekend to see her new baby; would you like to come round for spaghetti on toast?' Of course, Dot said yes without a moment's hesitation. She had been so astonished by what had happened that by the time they said goodbye her happiness was plastered across her face. She was desperate to tell the girls she worked with her news. The long wait for break-time was agonising. When they were finally allowed to leave the work place and go to the canteen, Dot told the girls everything. They wanted to know all the details: what Bob looked like, where he worked, where he lived. Some of the questions Dot couldn't answer because she didn't know Bob THAT well. Then they gave her all sorts of advice – don't let him do it on the first date but, if you do, make sure you're standing up. If you do it and you're not standing up, go to the toilet and have a pee. That usually flushes it out.

Dot kept Bob a strict secret from her mother; she would be bound to disapprove, which was why on the morning of her date with Bob she put on her sweetest face and reminded her she was going to be having tea at a workmate's house. Then one lie led to another and Dot said her friend had five baby kittens she wanted her to see, which made her mother completely forget about Dot going into unchartered waters and worry about the kitten she might bring home. It was when Dot was at work that she had a sudden fear her mum would start asking too many questions. She wanted nothing to spoil her evening with Bob and thought the best thing she could do was to catch the later bus. When Dot arrived home from work, her mother was standing on the front doorstep. She was about to ask why Dot was late, when Dot flew past her, saying, 'There's been a problem with the buses.' Without stopping, she hurried up the stairs and into her room, quickly changed out of her work clothes and put on a clean blouse and skirt. She picked up her bag, ran down the stairs as fast as her feet would take her, grabbed her coat and opened the front door, shouting, 'I'll be back by ten.' Dot didn't stop running till she got to the telephone booth. There was nobody in sight and she went into the booth, folded up the waistband of her skirt until it was an inch above her knees, took the tube of red lipstick from her bag, applied it to her lips, pulled out her comb and back-combed her fringe.

After Bob had given her his address, she had taken a walk past his house. It wasn't that she wanted Bob to see her; she'd hate him to think she was chasing after him. What she did want to know was how long it would take to get from her house to his. She had her wristwatch on and it took her exactly five minutes and fifteen seconds to the telephone booth, plus ten minutes and five seconds from the telephone booth to the house.

Dot arrived at Bob's house right on time. He was standing looking out of the downstairs window. He gave her a wave, left the window and seconds later the front door opened. Dot stepped into the house. Bob chatted as he took her coat and hung it on a coat hook. He was still chatting when she followed him into the kitchen, when she sat at the table and looked around her. All the council houses in their neighbourhood looked alike; if it wasn't for the numbers on the front doors it would be hard to tell one from the other. It was when you went into the houses that you saw their differences. Dot's mother loved brown. Everything in the house was brown or beige: the carpets, the three-piece-suit, even the shoes they wore. Bob's house was bright, with a mixture of colours that made Dot wonder if it was the reds and the yellows, the oranges and the pinks that gave the house its feeling of warmth, a comfortable place to be. Bob was still chatting when he filled the kettle and lit the gas-ring. Dot's eyes followed him as he went from cupboard to cupboard, collecting milk, teapot, sugar and mugs. As soon as the table was laid and the kettle had boiled he sat beside her and told her about his sister who lived in Birmingham with her husband and baby. Bob said his mum would want to see the baby often, which meant they would sometimes have the house to themselves. Nothing else was said about the matter, but Dot couldn't help thinking their relationship was more than a one-night stand.

The meal didn't take more than two minutes to get ready. The spaghetti was nice enough, though the white, sliced, toasted bread was a little overdone. Dot offered to help with the washing-up, and Bob said he would do it later. He invited her into the sitting room and Dot stood watching him draw the curtains together. Then he turned towards her, saying, 'We don't want anyone looking in at us, do we.' Dot felt Bob's arm slip around her as he led her to the sofa. She had never been or felt that close to anybody before, had made up her mind before she left home that Bob would be the one to take her virginity. She had no illusions about herself. She was skinny, her clothes were old-fashioned, and her hair was the colour of a dishcloth. She felt lucky that Bob was paying her any attention at all, that without him she would remain a virgin forever. Dot had never kissed anyone other than her mother and aunt. It was only when she met Bob that she started thinking about a different kind of kissing. Dot had practised kissing her reflection in her bedroom mirror. She could never be sure if her mouth should be partly or fully open, though she needn't have worried – when Bob put his mouth to hers they fitted nicely together.

Dot began to relax, enjoying the warmth of him, the taste of him travelling through her body. It was when he put his hand on her knee and it began to creep up her skirt that she thought she had some explaining to do. She didn't want to spoil the moment by saying "I think we'd better stand up" but she did say, 'I'm a virgin.'

Bob immediately took his hand away from her. She wondered what she had done wrong, that perhaps it was the way she kissed, and then he told her, 'Go home, Doris. You're a nice girl; find yourself a nice boy. Don't hang around with the likes of me.'

Dot was bemused when she stood up from the sofa. She felt the heat on her cheeks when he gave her her coat and opened the door. She heard the door close behind her, and a shroud of shame wrapped its way tightly around her as she walked home. She told herself that she had been under a misconception... the girls at work had told her boys liked going with virgins; it was something they prized. By the time Dot reached her house, she had made up her mind. She would dye her hair platinum blonde, raise the length of her skirts and pad out her bra. She would lose that thing called virginity at the first opportunity.

The changes came fast. Her mother thought Dot was had suffered from some kind of seizure, that a malady had besieged her. Dot didn't look like her Doris anymore, what with hair the colour of Marylin Monroe's, breasts that seemed to have appeared overnight and having to look up at her because of the ridiculous shoes she wore. Mrs Smith grew wary. If she'd known everything Dot had been up to, she would have died of shock.

* * *

I lost track of Dot shortly after, and she found a new group of friends. It was a few years later that I saw her again, when she happened to be in the Glen – a dance-hall not far from Bristol Downs. I wouldn't have recognised her if she hadn't spoken to me first. She was stunning. Her long, blonde hair fell past her shoulders; she was still very slim, but curvy in the right places. She told me her mother had given up trying to control her, that she was on the Pill, enjoying life and the freedom to do what she wanted. We were catching up on other things that had been going on when someone caught her eye. I heard her say, 'There's Bob,' and followed her over to him. The music was loud, but I heard her quite clearly shout in his ear, 'I'm not a virgin anymore!' ■

Thank you for reading – I hope you enjoyed these short stories!

If so, I would really appreciate it if you could share with friends and leave reviews.

You may also like to read my novels **Playinground** – set in the heatwave of 1976, and **Skylark** – a novel about loss, love and guilt. Both have received 5* reviews.

If you would like to stay in touch, I can be contacted on:

Twitter: @SusanHu76288306

Facebook: Susan Hutchins Author

and

Email: susanhutchins@gmail.com

Printed in Great Britain
by Amazon

79873732R00051